RAYMOND BRIGGS

Father Christmas

HAMISH HAMILTON

London

For my Mother and Father

HAMISH HAMILTON LTD

Published by the Penguin Group
27 Wrights Lane, London W8 5TZ, England
Penguin Books USA Inc., 375 Hudson Street, New York, New York 10014, USA
Penguin Books Australia Ltd, Ringwood, Victoria, Australia.
Penguin Books Canada Ltd, 2801 John Street, Markham, Ontario, Canada L3R 1B4
Penguin Books (NZ) Ltd, 182-190 Wairau Road Auckland 10, New Zealand.
Penguin Books Ltd, Registered Offices: Harmondsworth, Middlesex, England.

First Published in Great Britain in this miniature edition 1990 by Hamish Hamilton Ltd.

Copyright © 1973 by Raymond Briggs

1 3 5 7 9 10 8 6 4 2

British Library Cataloguing in Publication Data
CIP data for this book is available from the British Library

ISBN 0-241-130115

Printed and bound in Great Britain by
William Clowes Limited, Beccles and London

Father Christmas

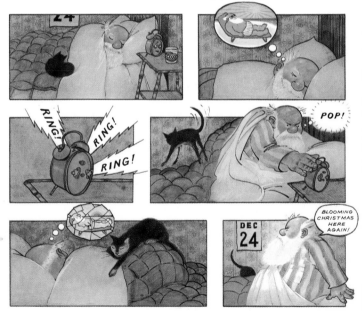

GET OFF MY SLIPPERS, DOG!

BLOOMING SNOW!

YAWN

I HATE WINTER!

HERE YOU ARE, DEERS.

GOOD POT OF TEA

BLOW THE BLOOMING SNOW!

THE FROZEN NORTH WILL BE VERY COLD—SNOW, ICE, SLEET...

BRRR!

GOOD GIRL!

KEEP STILL
YOU SILLY
DEERS !

GOODBYE CAT

GOODBYE DOG

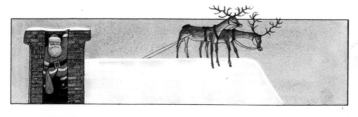

HM, BETTER THAN NOTHING I SUPPOSE.

🎵 HARK THE HERALD ANGELS SING 🎵

LOVELY PUD!

HM! PRESENTS! SEEN ENOUGH OF THOSE THINGS FOR ONE DAY.

NOTHING LIKE A GOOD BATH.

🎵 HARK THE HERALD ANGELS SING 🎵

NICE CLEAN SOCKS

GOOD DROP OF ALE.

LOVELY GRUB!

The End